Dog Park

Other books by David Jaicks

River Rock (2008)
Driving Home (2009)
Horses in the Fog (2012)
The Spirit Man (2014)
Road Dust (2015)

Dog Park

by David Jaicks

Special thanks to Jeanne Peck, Melissa Batalin, and Beth Craig.

Cover and book design by Melissa Mykal Batalin

Printed in the United States of America
The Troy Book Makers • Troy, New York
www.thetroybookmakers.com

To order additional copies of this title check with your favorite local bookstore, or contact the author directly at ***davidjaicks@gmail.com.***

ISBN: 978-1-935534-77-8

To Willy, the greatest gift of my life.

Getting There

If you ever drive into our town and you are at a light and you get behind a small pickup and the light changes but the pickup doesn't move, that's James and he is probably asleep. Don't worry though. He's got his foot on the brake and his truck probably won't drift. He claims he can tell the color of the light when it changes through his closed eyelids, but give him a gentle honk on your horn just in case.

You see James works nights at the college as a janitor. Sometimes he goes in when it's dark. It's a lonely job. He works alone, mopping and cleaning the locker rooms. Now and then security walks through but to him they sometimes seem like his jailors with their keys jangling and speaking in loud voices, leaving him alone to his thoughts, wondering what he has done wrong to deserve this.

He does get to bring his dog, Benny. Benny is a four-year-old Golden Retriever who used to follow James everywhere when he first started the job. But James darted around so much, forgetting to get enough rags or unplugging the vacuum that Benny has given up following and parks himself in the corner and sleeps.

In the morning, after James has returned home, slept, he still gets up early and goes out to his woodshop in his garage and starts working. He's not greatly accomplished at woodworking, but he owns a few machines and is always trying to get better at it. This summer he had taken on the challenge of trying to build a door for a family out in Illinois where James is originally from. The door is about done by now and he is pleased with it. It's not a fancy door, but he's decided to undertake this venture because it involves power tools he owns but avoids using because he has never really learned to use them right. This way, he figures he'll be forced to gain some familiarity.

He spends a few hours in there listening to the radio and sweating over his progress. Benny, once again, is parked outside and waits until this is over. Sometimes James wonders what Benny thinks he is doing in there. And sometimes James wonders what he himself is doing in there. He's not very good at woodworking, groping in the half light for his boards.

He had once made a chair that was tall and of thin design. No one ever sat on it for fear they would suddenly arrive on his floor. Most people pulled it close to them, balanced their cups, using it for a table. The chair had a strange appearance that seemed to look over the room like a Great Blue Heron in a pond.

After being in the woodshop, James usually puts Benny in his truck and the two drive over to the other side of town to the dog park. To get there though, they have to pass through the town, and then out past the airport.

James had always had a strange disconnection with the town. It seemed to be roughly divided between people who thought they owned the place, and those who didn't think the same way.

He certainly had contributed to their welfare. As a lifeguard he had once saved a little girl from drowning in a pool. Afterwards, the mother had gone up to him and said unappreciatively, "You really wanted to go in anyway, didn't you." James had thought about it for awhile and thought she was probably right. After many years of sitting beside a pool with not much to do, he had, at times, wished he could use his skills. But the mother probably would have also preferred he had gone in rather than not since she wasn't even in the room at the time.

And then on another occasion, James was driving down out from his house at night during a snowstorm. He had just moved in and all the new changes had seemed quite hypnotic and surreal. He came upon a rather bad traffic accident. A local girl had spun into a guardrail and lay slumped over her steering wheel. James was one of the first at the scene. A couple of guys were flagging traffic around her but she was alone in the car, unconscious, not breathing, with a bad head wound and sitting among blood and broken glass.

James wasn't sure exactly what to do, but he decided he would talk to her, try and reassure her. He thought some part of her might still be able to hear him among all the damage and trauma. As he held her hair out of her face, and stroked her gently, there was a sudden loud eruption as her shoulders shook and she started slow, heaving, gurgling breaths.

In awhile, the EMS arrived, and it may have been in the importance of saving her life but they pulled her out like she was a sack of potatoes. As they began to load her into the ambulance, James heard one say to another, "She started breathing when we got here."

This wasn't true. She started breathing when he got there. He knew how to recognize breathing especially when it was mixed with copious amounts of blood.

He probably should have been more aggressive about starting her breathing himself, but because of his own confusion from his new move, he hadn't had a good presence of mind, and at least she was on her way, and he felt he had contributed.

But still, James wasn't sure why there was this strange disconnection with the town. He had known of many people who had contributed to its well-being.

The problem also sometimes seemed based around economics. Some people seemed entitled to his money, what little there was of it. They showed this by overcharging him for their services and then not paying him much attention in any other way. James would think why should he support them for things, many of which he could do himself? He recognized the need for interdependence, but if he could do it himself, he would.

He had seen it in the business community as well. A newcomer might arrive, set up, and do quite well. The old crowd would become envious, and strive to make the newcomer unwelcome.

It was sort of sad, James thought. One group seemed to want more money while the other wanted friendship. But many of them had become his friends and there was enough there to keep him there. He thought he would let the chips fall where they may. He wasn't going to lose anymore sleep over it, but it did seem to cast, for him, a weird pall over the town. Maybe he'd write a book about it someday, he mused.

James had come to the area during his dark years, which had started even years before when he was in college. After graduating he had had trouble making it out of the starting gate, moved around a bit, and all he could think about was to keep moving around. He had heard about a place out east that might be able to help him, so he came out. The place turned out to be a good place, which he eventually left but continued to stay living in the area.

His sadness hadn't left him completely either. During his dark years, he once thought he'd try and buy a gun, and blow his head off. He started driving to the gun store to buy the gun.

While driving James was convinced that if God wanted James to stay around, the store would be closed or his car would break down on this way there. There would be some hindrance or intervention on the part of God to stop this process, and show James how much God wanted and needed him around. But as James crested over the top of the hill he looked down where a sign read, "Sale on guns today."

James immediately recalculated his thinking. He knew God was forgiving and all, but maybe God had nothing to do with it or James. So James turned his car around, realizing staying alive was going to be up to him, and so was his own happiness. After that his own life started to get better.

They got through the town and started to pass the airport. James always enjoyed going past the airport. He loved to see the small private planes parked out in the grass along the tarmac.

He had once heard a story from someone who was a jogger that had never been up in a small plane, but always wanted to. One day the man was out jogging on the road along the runway when a small plane passed him, taxiing out for takeoff. The jogger put out his thumb as a joke, for a ride. All of a sudden the plane spun around and the door opened. The jogger couldn't believe it but he finished his run that day flying over the hills and cornfields of the county.

When James and Benny got to the dog park, James exited his truck on the passenger side because the lock on his driver's side was busted. He slid across the front seat and opened the door. His water jug and portable radio fell out first, hitting the ground with a thud. He and Benny followed.

There were lots of people there with their dogs. Ken was there with his Portuguese Water Dog, Blue. Roland was there with his good natured Yellow Lab, and with Roland standing inside a bridal veil of dark mosquito netting. Jill was there with Rita who followed patiently after Jill like a student following her Zen master. Sal, the poet, was there walking shyly with her two Huskies, and bright with a smile. Bill and Linda were there with their ever popular Ginger, a black female Mixed Lab who got swallowed into the amoeba of dogs that surrounded her when she appeared at the gate. Right away Benny went over to Linda who was sitting and began dusting her with his tail. Since it was late July, the sun was bold. James set down in a chair and soon everyone else seemed to be sitting. The dogs were spinning like small tornados in front of them.

Benny, James's dog, ran up excitedly, dropping a tennis ball from his mouth, his tongue fluttering. This was James's signal. He bent down, picked up the ball and tossed it sideways into the center. The air was too hot to be throwing this ball, James thought as his blue jeans were quickly welding to his legs.

A car pulled up and a young woman sprang out. It was Claire. Everyone seemed to be excited to see her. James hadn't seen Claire in awhile and he too could feel his own heart beat, quicken as she approached them with her little dog, Maddy.

James first met Claire during the winter of that year. He had come to the dog park in his truck with Benny. It was afternoon and he was alone in the park standing in recent snow that had fallen from a bad storm the night before. No one was there because the weather was bad and because most people couldn't get in because their cars couldn't manage the conditions.

James would throw the ball to Benny and the ball would disappear into the snow. Sometimes Benny would find it, excitedly, his tail flickering while putting his nose under and sniffing. And sometimes he wouldn't and James would have to trudge down to the other end and kick and poke until a trace of yellow would appear among the frozen snow crust.

As James was there, he noticed car tracks that led to a car that had come in earlier and had been driven down a slope and abandoned. Its windows were open. It was a sobering sight, not just to see an abandoned car there, but James right away had another reason.

He started to get a sinking feeling he might be asked to help tow the car out. He could tell it was probably owned by some college kids who went to school in the area. The whole situation had a college-age look and feel to it and James wasn't pleased. He weighed the thought of escaping before anyone showed up, but stayed, continuing to throw and find the ball for Benny.

Pretty soon three college-aged women appeared, their jackets open, cheeks red. They waved to James and then hesitantly he drifted over to them and began asking a few questions. They explained they had tried to get the car out and couldn't. They had tried to call, but couldn't. Then they had tried to walk out a nearby road, but hadn't made it to a house. One young woman, the driver of the car, introduced herself to James as Claire.

"I knew this was a bad idea," she said, not quite meeting his gaze.

James lost track of the intricacies of their stories because he knew what he would be doing next and his whole afternoon was beginning to take a completely different shape than planned. But he also had a morbid curiosity of his own to see how his truck would perform. He hadn't yet tested it.

He agreed to help and backed his truck down to the front of Claire's car. At first they tied some scarves and old clothes to the front and attached onto James's bumper. The girls got behind to push. James accelerated, tires spun and the scarves and old clothing snapped right off.

They met again, conjectured. James had no rope but he pulled his jumper cables out from behind his seat and tied them on. The girls got behind. Claire steered. The tires spun. Engines raced and steamed. The cables stiffened, but not much happened with her car.

This went on for awhile. James found himself underneath their cars, readjusting, retying the cables. The snow was cold, had melted and his body was cold, and he was often at the point of giving up and giving them a ride into town for a wrecker, but they started to make a little progress. Each time they revved out they managed to gain a few feet and made it just enough for James to remain interested. They had spent a good hour and a half with maybe a third of the distance achieved, but they still had to make it to the crest of the hill.

James sat in his truck possibly to warm up when he suddenly had an epiphany. He had been using his four wheel drive option obviously, but he hadn't tried his low gear four wheel drive option.

He jumped out, motioned the girls to get back in position. Two weren't near and had to be rounded up like stray cattle because they had lost their faith. Soon he jumped back in, dropped it down and in one blast of spinning wheels, strained cables, broken scarves and shirts, the car slid sideways a bit but came back almost the whole way up from down in that hole.

Their vehicles appeared on the road. Claire jumped out. James jumped out. The other girls caught up. No one could really believe it had happened.

The girls stood around James thanking him. Claire gushed, "I'm taking you out to dinner.

What do you like?" James was pleased enough by the outcome and didn't want her to feel obligated.

"Don't worry about it," he said.

She tried to offer him some money. He refused. They said goodbye and drove away in separate directions. That was how James first met Claire in the winter.

Later James had run into Claire several times on the sidewalk in the town, at the bar, here and there. She had always had a smile on her face and was engaging towards him which he appreciated. He wasn't deluded that she liked him romantically. He was almost twice her age, but he appreciated her young female energy, and her interest in him seemed rare for a girl her age. He didn't know much about her, but he knew she wasn't in school but was thinking of going back to college. She always seemed to have a friend or two on her arm.

At the dog park she would pop in and out fairly quickly at first but as the summer went on she went through some changes it seemed and she got more comfortable with adults, and started to see herself as an adult as well.

James would go and the usual crowd was there, sometimes mostly men, some married and some not, and Claire would be planted right in the middle of them which they loved and the banter would be in full gear.

One of the men was a guy named, Pete. Pete had an unparalleled wit. He was personable to everyone but when the crowd was right, you couldn't get a word in edgewise because Pete's repeater was jammed and all you could do was lie down and hope you didn't get caught in his jokes that flew like bullets over your head.

Pete was married and had a restaurant and also raised money for an investment fund. Once in a while he spoke on a cell phone while they all sat together. And he said he was waiting to find out if he had raised fifty million dollars for his fund.

He made friends with other women who came to the dog park and sometimes they would drive off together. There was no reason to believe they were anything but friends, but James had no idea where they went except he had once heard that they had been down by the river, and someone came along and broke out the windows on their cars, and took some things. Pete also had a pool. Pete was liked by everyone though. James and Benny liked him, too. He always managed to seem to take an interest in them even though he was a bit over the top with his humor.

"How much for this lap dance, Ginger?" said Pete as one of the dogs climbed onto his chair, and licked him.

Claire once appeared at the dog park and James and Benny were the first she encountered as she went beyond to the chairs. She was always pretty, but on that morning James couldn't help notice her face was a blast of beauty and glow. She came right up to James and said, "Guess what? I'm moving to Boston. I'm going to go to art school and live with my sister." James smiled as she rolled past him like a flaming ball, sat down among the others and couldn't stop talking. At first James was a little sad. He thought he'd miss her. But as time went on, he reflected on her and thought it was good.

Claire was probably at a critical juncture in her life where she could make that break for college, make those friends and have those experiences that would aid her in ways during her life she at this point might never even have a clue about.

Even though he had trouble divorcing her from his mind, he started to see that this could be really good for her, and he threw Benny another ball.

Then one day James arrived with Benny in the heart of the summer heat. Everyone was there. Pete had the main bench with an open seat next to him. He was firing off jokes like artillery and his wife was there.

She was attractive and had a big smile and was keeping track of their dog who had some business that kept her from joining the rest of them.

Claire arrived, said hello to those on the outside and made her way into the interior of the group and sat down next to Pete. They greeted each other and talked a little among themselves. Then James saw Claire turn toward Pete and erupt.

"I don't know what I'm doing, Pete, right now and I can't say," she said, her voice filled with frustration. Then Pete turned back to her.

"I need to know," he snapped. "You don't know, but we all need to know."

Claire was working this summer as a hostess for Pete at his restaurant, and swimming at his pool. Pete needed to know if she was planning to keep her job with him or was she going to start college in the fall.

James surmised that in the short term, Pete's lifestyle probably seemed pretty alluring to Claire, the pool parties and whatnot and being a hostess wasn't a bad job, James thought. Lord knows he probably wouldn't be any good at it. And it probably tapped into one of Claire's qualities that they all exploited to some degree, her charm and ability to make people feel comfortable.

But it would be nice if she could have a shot at college. She could at least try it and test herself, James thought. As Pete left that day, James threw the ball out to Benny and the ball took a high arc over the park and for a moment looked like it was going to fall on Pete's head, but instead landed on a chair near him and made a loud clank.

James remembered a high school girl from the town he once knew who had gotten hired as a waitress at one of the restaurant town nightclubs. She was either going to take calculus that summer or work at the restaurant. One night she solicited opinions to a group sitting around the tables of the restaurant as to what they thought she should do. Some said work at the restaurant and some said go to school. She opted to work at the restaurant and every year that went by, James was sad to see her still there. She was with a different town boy each time, and eventually moved into the club where she became a barmaid of sorts. The last time James saw her she was slumped in a stairwell of a town bar, kissing someone and surrounded by a bunch of other guys. It smelled like pot. As James left, he nodded to one of the guys, who didn't nod back and just gave him a cold stare.

Claire had been in a mood that morning after talking to Pete. She and Sandy, who was very nice and who had a handsome Black Lab named Tanto, and James and Pierre went down to the river to swim their dogs.

The dogs all swam and ran on the bank. Pierre and Sandy were talking and James stood beside Claire and they talked. Claire said something about her dad being a high school teacher there.

"Really?" said James. "What did he teach?"

"History," said Claire, her eyes lighting up.

"What was his specialty?" asked James.

"American," said Claire, "and some European."

"Did he know Haidek?" James asked. Haidek was another teacher he had known who had taught at the school.

"Oh sure," said Claire. "He knew Mr. Haidek. They taught together."

"Sam Haidek?" said James, "Right?"

"Yes," said Claire, "Sam Haidek. My dad often joked about affairs between students and teachers in the old days." They both laughed.

"They were younger then," said James. "And times were younger," Claire nodded.

"What do you do for Pete?" James asked, not being certain.

"I'm a hostess," said Claire, her shoulders deflating. "At Osprey. Last night we seated a hundred people." Sandy and Pierre started to walk out to their cars. James and Claire started to follow.

"Are they still seated?" James said, joking. Claire smiled and her mouth twisted.

"Yah. They're still waiting for their dinner."

Thank God for a Woman's Voice

There were nights when he'd be working alone mopping a floor or cleaning a sink or a toilet and James would hear a woman's voice come on the radio. It had seemed too long since he had heard one. He liked men, but women never really seemed to be around.

His mom had died when he was in his twenties. He never had sisters. He only had a brother and a dad.

He had dated some and there had been plenty of mistakes. That was for sure. But nothing had seemed to work out. He often was alone. It was good to hear a woman's voice he had thought on those nights. Thank God for a woman's voice he had thought. And sometimes he put his head in his hands and wondered sadly.

One time James came to the dog park and there was a small group gathered and trying to hide in the small puddle of shade as the sun beat down like a sledge hammer.

One of the women there had long dark hair, pulled back, sat upright on the bench, and beneath her arms was a big round belly. Her name was Davita and she was seven months pregnant. She spoke softly and he liked hearing her voice which was as soft and gentle as the wind.

She said she was from Russia and had come here alone, although she had an uncle here. She had met a young guy who had gotten her pregnant and they were living together in an apartment in a nearby town. Back in Russia she had studied international relations in school, but hadn't finished and was now here with a guy she wasn't sure she wanted to marry, and was carrying his child. Her voice was of dismay which also included dismay for America.

As she spoke, James became aware of a great sadness in her and soon realized it wasn't the average conversation he had had at the dog park.

He sat up in his chair, listened, and continued to throw the ball to Benny. Soon, though, there was the sound of car doors slamming as some new people were arriving.

"What would you like to do?" he said, rushing his words because the privacy of their conversation would soon be ending.

Davita sighed and looked over at him. "I don't know," she said. "I just want to go back to Russia to raise my baby and be near my mother."

As James got to know Davita over the course of the summer, he always enjoyed hearing her soft voice but he was always aware of her great sadness which seemed to lay over her like a veil.

Sometimes James would arrive at the dog park and Davita would be sitting out there alone, her arms at her side beside her big belly as prominent as the moon. Her little dog, Lecha, would be sniffing at the ground beside her.

James would carefully enter with Benny, walk over, sit down, start throwing the ball out to Benny. He was always ready to listen.

As far as Davita's boyfriend was concerned, James didn't' know. She had never said what he had done, or what might be wrong.

James didn't know if it was the boyfriend, or some immaturity around motherhood, or her dissatisfaction with America, or some or all of these factors combined that was weighing on her. But James didn't press her on it.

James had seen her with the boyfriend once in a bar in town. James had walked in and she was sitting at the end of a table, her back straight and upright like she was at the dog park, only she looked quite solemn.

The boyfriend was along the side of the table, sitting with friends. James saw the white flash of his smile, his back against the wall.

James remembered meeting Pierre for the first time at the dog park. Pierre wasn't a tall man but he was built like a Volvo. He had had a French accent and wouldn't stop talking about cooking.

He worked at the community college, teaching cooking classes and he catered various events around town. He was a French immigrant and his little dog was named Bona Petite.

Pierre wasn't boring. He was fun to listen to. But James sometimes thought, man, this guy sure could talk a blue streak about asparagus and noodles.

Once James was in his woodworking shop, listening to Pierre speaking on the local radio station. James couldn't remember much about what he said but he remembered Pierre praising the Portuguese because of their frequent use of the tomato.

One morning James pulled up at the dog park and he and Benny joined both Davita and Pierre and the others. They were sitting together on the bench and Pierre was talking about cooking, French cooking. He went on and on and they were all starting to get a little hungry as they got into the cuisine served at the local restaurants. Pierre wasn't holding back about his praise or criticism of certain places.

James began to wonder what batteries Pierre seemed to run on that most people didn't have.

Then something magical happened. Pierre asked Davita what kind of cooking her mother served.

"What do you mean?" Davita spit back.

"What did she serve on Sunday?" asked Pierre.

There was a moment of silence and then as if a cloud had moved past the sun, Davita's demeanor started to change. She thought for another moment and a smile started across her face.

"Borscht with apples and beans," she said. "We always had borscht with apples and beans. After church, even when we didn't go," she laughed out quietly with a little guilt, her eyes starting to twinkle as she remembered.

"How many were there of you?" said Pierre.

"There were five of us," she said. "Wait." She looked down at her fingers quickly and counted.

"Yes, five," said Davita. "The three of us and our parents."

By now people were starting to smile at Davita's face that was filling with color. All their chairs were turned toward the two of them. She called out to James.

"Hey James? What kind of Russian cooking do you like?" James snapped out of his trance.

"I don't know? Beef Stroganoff?" he said.

"Is that what you think Russian cooking is?" said Davita laughing. "There is so much more."

This happened several other times as well. Everyone would be there and Pierre would be excitedly talking about food, his head boiling over with enthusiasm. Davita would be smiling and they all would laugh. Pierre was kind of like a therapist. And afterward, some of them would take their dogs down to the river for a swim.

Once James brought Benny in and Benny got into a terrible scuffle. A Wheaten Terrier had arrived and as James reached out to shake the hand of the Wheaten's owner James suddenly saw out of the corner Benny and the Wheaten combust into a fudge twirl of fighting red and blond fur.

James had to step in and fend off the other dogs who now all wanted a piece of Benny as well.

When they left that day James drove down to the river with Benny. Pierre was there with Bona Petite. It was nice and peaceful. They threw sticks out to their dogs and Pierre didn't once say a word about food.

Every morning James would also return back to his woodshop. It was kind of a refuge for him. He was continuing to make progress on the door, and thought he would finish it soon.

He pulled his router out and began to run it across a board. Suddenly the router jumped as James had hit a change in the grain and wood splintered out.

James thought of his good friend, Randy, who was a contractor and who James had even worked for.

Randy used to say "A good carpenter is not someone who never makes mistakes. A good carpenter knows how to fix his mistakes, because we all make mistakes."

But James looked down at the gash in his board and thought, I don't know how I'm going to fix this one. I wish you were here.

James often wished Randy was following him around in his shop as he stumbled over the waste ends and sawdust of his cut boards, Randy telling him what to do like an excited coach.

Benny on the other hand was a little confused around James' involvement with his woodshop. Benny didn't really understand what James was doing in there and nothing about it seemed too dog relevant.

After Benny's meter had expired, James would see a damp tennis ball roll into view, and lightly breaded with sawdust. This meant that James should give up the machinery and noise and join the real world.

Another Use for a Newspaper

They had been sitting around most of the early morning. It had been a good morning. Almost everyone was there. The familiar faces, snouts, and tails. Carol and Tim were there. Both had grey hair and usually wore black. They were like salt and pepper shakers as they stood together on the high ground overlooking their dogs.

Carol was a teacher and during the summer had taken on the responsibility of being the informal manager of the dog park. She collected donations and made sure the garbage cans were emptied. She had spent her winters managing a classroom of rebellious high school teens so she was certainly capable of handling the dog park in the summer. James thought those of us who were aware of her and her service were quite grateful.

When Carol left she wished everyone that morning "to have a great day," which was well meaning, but James mused to himself a little cynically what a "great day" would be to him.

He thought he might open his mail, and find it full of nothing but big checks, all written out to him. Then he would walk into town to the bank to deposit them and as he passed the gas station a guy would call out, "Hey, do you want my car? I don't need it anymore. Go ahead. It's even got a full tank." Then as James was pulling out a woman would run up to him and say, "My husband just left me and I need you." And they would drive off together to an undisclosed location.

Just then as James awakened from this fantasy he looked up and saw Benny assuming his pooping position as if Benny was sitting in a rocking chair. This simple achievement, thought James, would make his day great enough. He pulled a bag from his pocket and began walking in Benny's direction.

As he walked he passed Sal, the poet who was there with her two Huskies. James said hello and thought she was probably thinking something poetic.

Davita arrived and got slowly out of her car, her big belly causing her to list to one side. Pete called to her.

"Hey Davita, you better leave your engine running."

"Why?" someone said.

"In case she starts to go into labor," Pete joked.

Claire had arrived and sat down next to Davita who had made her slow way over to the bench. Claire had her head against Davita's belly as she listened. Suddenly Claire sat up and her eyes were like stars.

"I just felt him," said Claire. Davita smiled and looked down.

"My baby has the hiccups," said Davita.

"Really?" said Claire.

"Yes," said Davita, smiling.

James walked further away to clean up after Benny.

Benny was a good dog and always had a way of not making things too difficult for James. When he arrived in James' life, James felt lucky, as though he had inherited a beautiful farm. Benny was the best dog James had ever known and his upkeep and care kept James' mind off himself.

As James went off to throw away the bag, he heard a high pitched scream, and the sounds of others in concern. At first he thought some dogs were in a fight or yelping. He looked back and saw people gathering around Davita who was now lying back with her legs up and Jill was fanning her in big, broad sweeps with the local newspaper.

People were running around Davita and a small crowd had gathered. James ran back to see what he could do.

"What happened," he said.

"It's Davita and her water has broken," Jill answered. James looked down and saw the bench was glistening and shinning where Davita had been sitting.

"Should we call out for help?" said James.

"Good idea," said Ken, and James started out of the crowd, passing Pierre who knelt beside Davita and was smoothing her forehead with a damp cloth.

Davita looked up at the sky and her chest was heaving. She groaned.

It seemed that most of them didn't know what to do. The usual nurses and retired nurses weren't present. Some of the usual loud mouths also seemed the most clueless, standing in the background conjecturing, their hands in their pockets, arms folded.

Ken had once heard that some of the obscure sections of a newspaper were good material to receive a baby in because they hadn't been touched by human hands and were quite clean. So he managed to interrupt Jill's fanning and set aside the sports section.

"What do you think we ought to do?" Ken asked out loud. Right then Sal, the poet, came bounding in. She knelt between Davita's legs, lifted Davita's dress up and began to feel around Davita's interior.

"The baby is coming," Sal looked up and announced. Davita's breathing had grown heavy and Sal bent her legs higher. "Alright Davita," she said, "This isn't going to be easy, but I want you to push. Push, Davita, push!"

Most people had never even heard Sal speak let alone suddenly move in and take command of the birth center.

"Push, Davita, Push!" Sal shouted.

James was now running to the gate to get to his truck to make that call on his cell phone. He reached the second chain link handle, lifted it and the last gate closed behind. He ran to his truck, grabbed for his cell phone and began calling.

"Hi. I'm at the dog park and we have a birth going on. No, it's a human birth. A young woman is giving birth..."

James looked back at the crowd. Everyone was huddled around Davita and it looked as though someone in a white shirt was giving her a bear hug. James turned back and finished the call. He hung up and grabbed a bandana out of his cab. He didn't know what it could be used for, but he grabbed it anyway. He started back inside the gate. He lifted the handle and one door closed. He lifted the handle of the next, and as it started to close, James heard a sound he had never heard before at the dog park. At first he thought a dog was in trouble, or some birds were squawking. But it was the sound of an infant, crying. He looked up. Davita had delivered a baby boy. The gate softly closed behind him.

James approached the group more slowly now. Everyone was crying. The baby who was wrapped in the sports section of the local newspaper was now cradled in Pierre's arms who was rocking him gently and already speaking to him about the merits of French cuisine.

Way out in the middle of the park, James sat down on the ground, took his hat off and looked out at the trees.

Good God, he thought. What a morning. He had no idea what time it was or where Benny was, or where anything really was. He was spent. He swept the sweat off his face with the shoulder of his shirt and looked out at the trees. He was a little contemplative, a little sad.

All that time trying to adjust yourself to a new life, he thought. All that time not knowing. No wonder some women who are pregnant get depressed, he thought. All that time not knowing who is inside you, or what it will be like.

The hardest part for Davita now was over, it seemed to him. At least now she could put her thoughts into action.

Claire came up and sat down next to James.

"She'll probably make a fine mother," he said as he looked out at the trees. "She seems to have taken it seriously."

Claire nodded. They both looked off at the forest.

"Pete was the hero of the day," said Claire with some surprise.

James looked over at her and said, "What do you mean?"

It turned out Pete had gone to medical school when he was young and studied obstetrics. He dropped out, though, for unknown reasons and had become a lawyer instead.

During Davita's delivery, Pete had been keeping a low profile, standing in the back with Roland and the others. When he saw that Davita's baby was slightly breached, Pete had stepped in, gave her a slight chiropractic move that changed her position and the baby had slid out as clean and easy as poop from a dog.

Pete was now being hailed as the hero of the day by several of the older men.

"I didn't know you were an obstetrician," said Roland.

"I'm not," said Pete. "But I wish I could hand out cigars. Here have a dog biscuit instead."

James looked over at the mob surrounding Davita. Davita was still lying back. She had a strange serene expression on her face. She looked up at the sky and said something softly in Russian. Jill poured water gently over her forehead.

"Go figure," James said eventually to Claire.

"Are you still planning to move to Boston?" he asked.

"Yes," she said.

"Yahoo," said James and threw his hat up and then caught it.

In a minute, Claire looked at him.

"Sure is hot. Want to take the dogs swimming?" she said. "I might jump in myself."

"Yes, but I don't have a suit," James said.

"I don't have one either," Claire said, "but it's not going to stop me." James smiled.

"You know how to make an old man lose his train of thought," he said.

"You're not that old," said Claire, exaggerating her words.

They decided James would drive. They walked out to his truck, loaded the dogs in the back.

Claire started to climb into the cab, but James pulled her back by her shirt.

"I have to get in first," he said, a little embarrassed. "My lock is busted on the driver's side."

"You got to get that thing fixed," she said.

"I know," he said as he entered on her side and she followed. They drove slowly away just as the ambulance to take Davita and her new baby away pulled into the driveway.

Saying Goodbye

Some time passed and some things had changed. The door was finished. James was happy with it. He had mastered the router well enough so that only the bit would spin and not his whole garage.

At the college where James worked, security still came through at night with their keys jangling but they seemed less like his jailors and more like friends. They even stopped and talked occasionally.

And as far as the town seemed he had started to see it as a collection of individuals and not one solidified whole. Most of them were a product of guess work that his own outlook could effect either way he chose.

But James decided he would move back to Illinois.

His job at the college was ending. His dad was elderly and might need a hand getting around. James wasn't sure what he would do but he had the phone number of a guy who said he needed carpenters.

One day James packed up his woodworking machines into the back of a rental truck. He slid the new door in. The next day he packed up everything else and on the next day he and Benny began the long drive west.

On his way out he thought he would stop at the dog park to exercise Benny and to say goodbye for one last time.

He pulled the caravan alongside the park and managed to get out with Benny beside him. The sky was cloudy. There was a chill to the air. Fall was coming on.

There weren't a lot of folks there, and strangely it was no one he recognized. He threw the ball to Benny who returned each throw with his usual enthusiasm and glamour of shining fur. But James was aware of the time and thought they better get an early jump on the trip. They had an eight hundred mile drive ahead of them.

As he started to walk out, he looked back at the place where they all used to sit and stand. He blurred his eyes, and for a moment, they all came alive again in front of him.

Ken was getting up from his chair, with his back bent like the older man that he was. Bill and Linda were calling out to Ginger, Bill with his big grin and gentle, smiling eyes behind his gray mustache. Sal was off to the side looking up at the trees.

James began to smile to his friends. He had realized that just as Davita had given birth, so had he to himself. He was a different person now. He began to raise his hand to wave goodbye, but as he did they all vanished like old ghosts, as quickly as morning fog. He and Benny walked out and for the last time, the last gate closed behind.

They started driving down the old gravel road. Then out to a faster road. James was both happy and sad. He had come to this place a long time ago for help which he had found as well as many friends. But it was time to go on to a new place or an old place in a new way.

He looked down at Benny who looked back with his little brown eyes like watermelon seeds. Then he looked up at the sun which had just put its head on the shoulder of a cloud.

He had never been much of a praying man but he looked up at the sky and said a few words of thanks.

He pulled the rental truck onto an even faster road and soon the long caravan was merging onto the interstate as a big semi tracker trailer sped by, sucking them both into its trail.

A Reminiscence

Over the years past James had taken many trips back to see his father. Many times he had driven, but many times he had flown because the drive had become so arduous. Each time his father seemed a little less present like the last of a shrinking snow.

Each time James flew he passed over Lake Michigan and James would gaze from his window over the dark slate water that came under the belly of the plane.

What a confusing body of water, he thought. It had brought so much pleasure to him when he was young.

He remembered being a child, and awoken by his mom before dawn as she excitedly bustled him off into the back of a station wagon filled with family, friends, food and an iron frying pan. They were to watch the sun rise from a beach and cook breakfast.

James remembered goose bumps on his legs from the cold as they ran in the shadows and turning waves. Then, as if a kettledrum was playing in their heads, the big red orange sun would appear, pulling itself above the horizon. They would cook bacon and fry eggs in the grease in the frying pan over a driftwood fire. The kids would swim and bury each other in the sand, the same sand his ancestors buried their tea service in as their own family escaped along the shore during the great Chicago fire, with their possessions.

The same sand he climbed a bluff from with friends as a young man, kicking the coals of a fire over the top edge to light the bluff's face as they practiced rappelling in the black night. And finally, the same sand many rescuers left from to search for a beloved cousin who had ventured out bravely with his two daughters in a boat into the lake, but was never found.

Such a confusing place James thought as the planes drifted in over the water. He was always glad to be back on the tarmac among the ballet of small ground vehicles and parked planes being nursed by fuel hoses and attendants. Lake Michigan was both thrilling, but so tragically tragic for him.

The Goodness Of The Pines

Civil Disobedience

"In this act of civil disobedience I am protesting the excessive layer upon layer of laws enacted by federal, state and municipal governments of our country that now seem to restrict the freedom and happiness of its own people.

"I haven't blown apart a federal building filled with innocent victims. I haven't formed a militia with the intent to do undue harm. I have just tried to go swimming with my dog."

Then, almost as soon as this statement was made by James, he lay back in the cool canvas of clear water and two pairs of arms reached down and jerked him up into the hot sun along the shores of Lake Michigan.

They were policemen and one said immediately, "You're under arrest for violating the Granville City dog beach code 797845. No swimming at the dog beach with your dog."

A woman cheered as he was led away, and several people weren't sure what was happening. They thought it might be a rehearsal for a commercial because there was no film equipment present. James looked over at the woman who cheered and he started to raise his fist in defiant solidarity, but he suddenly realized she may be cheering that he was being arrested.

Before they loaded James and Benny into the police car, the police stopped and put on their shoes and socks. When they got back over to the car they bent James' head down to clear the roof, and had trouble with Benny whose tail kept protruding in the way of the closing door. The car eventually sped away.

It was ninety degrees out. They rounded the corner by Burger King, its rooftop smoking with the smell of fried burgers. There had been swimming at beaches to the left and right of him, James thought. It only seemed natural that he could lay down in the cooling waters with his dog.

Things had gotten too tight. His apartment was full of loose coins he needed to quench the thirst of the parking meters that stood all over the city like planted trees. The parking officers were like Nazis. They drove around in little blue Toyotas, their defenses up and knife-like, if you crossed them.

He also started to miss his old home in the east. He thought of the dog park and forested hills. He had had a taste of the wilderness of the city. Maybe this act of civil disobedience would send him back in the direction of his home.

He still had his house which he knew would take forever to sell in the gloom of the economy. The dog park would still be there. And maybe they would take him back at the college. He had had a kind of elastic relationship with them that he was most grateful for.

As he paid his two hundred dollar fine for swimming with his dog at the dog beach, he walked out of the police station with Benny, into the hot sun, a free man, again.

The door had been hung, painted, and functioned perfectly fine as a door. The family was pleased and glowed with satisfaction over it. James said goodbye to his dad who was elderly but who didn't really need him yet, could manage fine on his own because of his blessed caregivers, and who didn't really seem to want him around anyway, would rather see him off on his own, continuing his own life for himself. James had promised to visit often as he had done regularly.

James packed up his small factory of equipment and started back east with Benny. His journey he had made many times now, went like a machine as he automatically traveled east in the direction of the rising sun. He arrived at his house and as he opened the door it seemed to kiss the new air like opening the tight seal on a refrigerator.

James got his job back at the college. One night as he was getting off from work, James walked out into the dark parking lot still twinkling from winter salt. Benny immediately broke into a run and soon they were throwing the ball again that sometimes would drop over a hill.

The ball disappeared and Benny disappeared and there was a moment when James wondered if he would ever see the two again. But soon they reappeared, the little yellow ball inside Benny's mouth like a forgotten star.

Shortly thereafter on another night James was hungry so he went into town for food. Small groups of people lingered in the street. James parked his truck and the sound of the door closing echoed through the canyon of small buildings.

A bartender named Frankie stood outside a local bar smoking a cigarette, his back and one foot against a brick wall. He blew out smoke and looked up into the sky. As James approached, Frankie nodded, then threaded his way back in through a crowd and reappeared behind the bar.

"What can I get cha'? he said.

"Can I get some food?" James asked.

"Sorry. Kitchen's closed," said Frankie. "Closes at ten."

"Thanks," said James and walked out, crossing the street to another bar restaurant.

It was late for food. The waitresses from all around town were starting to collect in one spot like phosphates in the eddy of an ever slowing river. A group sat at two tables outside a new restaurant that stood freshly painted and lit like the theatrical set of a play.

James nodded and said hello to some familiar faces, and inquired about food. They were skeptical about his chances of getting any at this time, but their friendliness made him remain.

He stood and listened as a well liked local drummer spoke of having to have part of his skull removed two summers back, and scrubbed because of an infected root canal.

James listened with compassion as the conversation wandered a little, eventually winding down to an old familiar topic in a small town.

"You see that store down there with the blue sign?" said the drummer. "I used to get my hair cut in there for five dollars. Now its a woman's boutique full of ladies dresses all a different shade of purple."

"I know," someone else said. "I used to get parts for my car here. Now it's a restaurant."

Everyone laughed and James smiled. Things always change, he thought, and started to think about food again, eyeing the curve of a rib bone on a plate like a washed up ship.

His quest for food was starting to look as though he was going to have to drive out to the turnpike where there were two restaurants open all night long. Or perhaps the warmth and good company of these people would feed him enough.

James said goodnight, and returned to Benny who was asleep in the truck and smelling the smells of a late night town along a river.

In These Hills

Before returning to the dog park that morning, James pulled into the country store for a snack. He went inside, said hello, and then drew a cinnamon bun from inside its case and paid at the wooden counter.

Just as he was leaving a friendly discussion broke out between the owner and his wife about the monument on the corner. This area was filled with history and it wasn't a surprise to see a pyramid of soldered cannon balls and a plaque here and there.

It turned out that General Corkeran, a colonial war general had passed through the area during one of his campaigns. James overheard the man say to his wife, that Joe Wilson, a neighbor, had dug up some cannon balls on his lawn and asked a local politician, who was a friend, to have the monument moved to his property. The politician agreed, so the monument was moved.

James smiled and they both looked over at him but he wasn't about to enter into the conversation. History was subjective, he believed, and he wasn't going to let anyone or anything get between him and the cinnamon bun right then.

The Story of Jupiter

James appeared again inside the fences of the dog park. He found himself standing among a herd of stampeding Labradors. Benny was glad to be back it seemed. His enthusiasm had not waned. As usual he was focused and serious about his pursuit of the bouncing tennis ball.

A woman pulled up in a small truck that resembled an armored car. She had been attending the mornings and James had spoken with her a little during the summer. She was a farmer who slaughtered her own beef but she was carefully dressed and usually held a thermos of green tea close to her chest as she moved about creating a constellation of travel, choosing not to mix too closely with many people. She seemed a little reticent but everyone had their way of joining. Some were more like Labradors, doing it quickly with their tails wagging. Others preferred to be careful.

She had a beautiful young gray male Weimaraner who was all heart and bounded with unbridled love. He rarely fought, and his back legs seemed to operate independently from his front legs as he ran good naturedly toppling into a crowd of standing dogs. His name was Jupiter.

James had always felt a bond with the woman. He respected her independent way and because her dog had never been neutered. Neither had Benny. Both dogs seemed agreeable, and maintained affectionate relations with themselves and others and managed to escape the common religious belief that we must neuter all our animals without question.

James could see it for many situations, but he wasn't convinced that it was for all, and had managed to raise Benny to five years without too many problems. But a deeper reason existed beyond that.

The woman appeared in James' range. They greeted each other and commented on the beauty of the morning. Then the woman announced that Jupiter had an appointment on Thursday to be neutered.

James' heart sank. Here was this good natured, young dog so full of love and well-meaning energy about to be altered. He thought about him, his radiance and he started to question her quietly.

"I don't know," she said. "It seems like he should have it done."

Benny's own fortune had seemed like a gamble among this stern climate, but he had done alright so far. To lose Jupiter this way saddened James.

James continued to speak with her and his own degree of passion surprised him. She couldn't bring up too much that seemed substantive, but that had nothing to do with her, she was certainly capable. It may have been that she too had been surprised by James' reaction. A small group was standing and watching and listening and when James walked away his head was in a mist laden cloud.

Several days passed and James hadn't slept well. Then in the early morning of that Thursday, James awoke and lay thinking. A picture of Jupiter came into his mind. He saw the happy dog in the sun; his back legs continuing to run while his front legs had stopped, causing him to jackknife like a truck into a crowd of playing dogs.

Then he thought of something else. He thought of a job he had had as a boy. He had left home, during a summer as a teen and hitch-hiked a good section of the country. In South Dakota, he had worked on a farm as a hired hand. It was a hog farm. He lived in the hired hand's house and worked with another hired man and the farmer during hot days among hog pens and acres and acres of healthy corn. One of his jobs was to castrate the baby pigs. He could still hear the hired man say, "C'mon James. Let's go out and cut some pigs."

There was no modern way to do this then, except to get out your pocketknife.

He tried to explain this to a friend once and she asked, "Why do they castrate pigs?"

"I was told they get ornery in their pens with each other," said James.

Once James remembered they had to castrate an adolescent pig. It had one testicle that had been overlooked and the farmer had spotted him later in a pen of desperate, hungry pigs. The pig seemed to know they were coming for him and James had to hold him down while they cut.

James cried out and sat up in his bed that early morning. He thought about that time and it had returned to him often and with such horror that he now thought he knew why he felt such strength over the issue. But like so many things in life he had to accept even though he didn't want to.

Later James made it back to the dog park with Benny. Pete had arrived that morning telling jokes and wearing a green fishing hat with a tail of an orange feather sticking out of its band.

James listened to Peter, laughed and began feeling better. Somehow Pete's jokes sat alright with James and James decided Pete wasn't such a demon afterall. At the outset James hadn't known Pete well enough to draw lines around him. His involvement with Claire and the restaurant was just a small wave on an otherwise fairly smooth sea of goodness, a sea that kept many afloat on Pete's humor.

Claire appeared from Boston that morning. She wore a white and yellow rabbit fur coat and a stairway of hair that flowed onto her shoulders. She looked like a movie star, and was immediately surrounded by men and women who pinned her to the fence wanting to know about Boston. Some of them lived vicariously through the presumed success of her adventures.

She held tightly to her privacy at first but as her visit progressed, she relaxed and bits of information leaked out.

James left before he could ask many questions and learn enough. He was happy to see her filled with glow and that her fire was still burning. As he drove away he was glad the balance of life was still present.

Dark Star

The winter lay its white blanket over the dog park and the tracks of dogs and people took different patterns, receded and returned like the glaciers of so many centuries. And then one day the sun shone, the snow melted and the grass greened beneath an endless sky tickled by pines.

James pulled up at the dog park to give Benny a run before work. A young woman was sitting on the bench far off. He saw she was with a little boy who was near her sitting on the ground, like a jug, and smoothing the grass beside her.

James realized who she was immediately. She was Davita with her son, and as he approached her, her dog and a tall figure stepped out from behind a small triangle of trees behind them. The young man had a piece of grass in his smile.

"Hello, James," she called out.

"Hello Davita," James replied, and nodded to the young man who joined Davita and her son from the side.

"James, this is Paul," said Davita and the young man held out his hand which James shook and a shimmer of wind went through the birches behind them causing an applause among their leaves.

"Hello," said James and smiled at the small family that seemed to have weathered their first seasons together.

"And this," said Davita as she bent down to pull a slime-covered ball from the hands of the little boy, "is Bjorn."

James knelt and grinned.

"How was your winter, James?" asked Davita.

"Long, but fine," said James. "And yours?"

"We got through it," she said smiling up at Paul.

After a moment James said, "Well that bench you are sitting on sure has some meaning to your little family."

"It certainly does," said Paul, chiming in. "I heard all about it."

"Maybe we should enshrine it in a museum?" said James, joking.

James walked out that day happy about Davita, her intact family, and the friendliness of her partner Paul. He decided to take the lazy slow road to work; Benny seemed to have no objection.

The Experiment

After many seasons of chasing dogs and tennis balls, the dogs had become friends, and so were some of the people. So someone finally suggested there ought to be a party.

James arrived during a late summer evening, pulled up in his truck and looked out at the gathering of people and dogs brightly dressed and decorated. A German Shepard named Sasha wandered the perimeter in front of him wearing a pointed party hat, and balloons tied around her collar.

James exited his truck and Benny spilled onto the ground. James gripped tightly to his contribution which was a box of store bought chocolate chip cookies.

"I see you are sticking to your bachelor nature, James," said Carol laughing out as she watched him sheepishly make his way in through the gates.

"Yes," said James, embarassed. "I'll help wash dishes," he said knowing he was being a bit of a scoundrel for bringing just the cookies.

The clouds had smoothed above them, the sunset putting an orange glow onto the surrounding forest. Benny seemed to disappear behind some trees as James wobbled over to the group which was gathered around two central people.

Beth and Kris were sitting and trying to talk, laugh and eat while fending off several food enthusiasts who happened to have four legs each and tails decorated with streamers.

"Joe! Keep his tail out of the dip!"

"Cash!" shouted Joe who rose suddenly to keep his dog from fanning the onion dip off the top of the picnic table.

"And then..." said Kris while still talking as she stood to become taller than everyone's dog who now wanted a bite of her cold enchilada. "...All you could do was keep hoping," she said, explaining certain weather problems during a recent trip to India.

People were trying to listen and tell stories and a dog would leap up for a lick of pâté or a bite of stromboli, and the person would pirouette out of the conversation, cursing.

"You wouldn't believe what we all went through," said Beth returning to her postion at the table.

James and Benny started to move off into a dark orbit around the park, looking back at the cars and dogs and people.

This was an experiment that might require greater introspection, James thought, as he considered the idea of meeting under a sunset with dogs and dinner and people.

Uncomplicated Reasons

A week went by and James found Benny needed to see someone other than James so he scooted his little truck back across town to the dog park with Benny. No one was there. It was afternoon and the sun had lowered to a shelf above the trees.

He threw the ball to Benny until he was tired. Then his eye caught a glint of gold shining from the bench where they all had sat by the trees.

He walked over and saw a broad bronze plaque attached to the top rib of weathered wood. Surprised, he bent to read. It said, "Bless this bench, this park, this place. Dogs are imprecise. People are worse. But that's why we like them."

A smile shot across James' face like a hunting arrow. He could easily hear Peter, Roland, and Ken saying these words. Or he could hear Bill or Jill or Claire or Davita or any of them really, speaking them out as well. Even the whole wide world for that matter. Because dogs are dogs and people are people and that they often should belong together. There was nothing wrong with this place. He looked off over the territory of the park, the hallowed ground.

James threw the ball out to Benny but his exuberance made the ball bounce out of the park and onto the road.

Damn, he thought. Extra leg work. But there was another summer staring at him. It seemed to roll out ahead like a long pink tongue. A summer of mosquitoes, and barking and bouncing balls.

James and Benny started out through the last gate that was closing behind them. James kicked at it and missed. The last gate closed anyway, bumping him and sending them on their way.

Toby

The years came and went happily and then a sad day arrived. Benny died in the spring of his ninth year. Benny had been diagnosed with a mass in his chest. After many visits to vets and surgery his mass spread to other parts of his body. One day and evening it became clear to James he was now going to lose his friend forever.

James would throw the ball ten feet from Benny, but his dog could no longer walk in the snow to get the ball. James pleaded with God and Benny to try and help him, but Benny could only stand in the snow, his legs bent inwards like a calf.

The vets let James go forward with the procedure to end Benny's life outside their building. After helping to hold the syringe that held the chemical that would stop Benny's heart, James lay sprawled over his friend in a patch of snow and sobbed. There were spring birds in the trees nearby singing. But James could only feel the still warm body of Benny against his chest as he lay over him.

Benny was the best dog James had ever known.

James spent a sad year and longer grieving for his lost companion. He found himself welling up with tears at the thought of him gone, and was often alone and he even became combative with some of the people who had agitated him and had to catch himself before things got out of hand. But as time heals, it had also been true for James.

People suggested he try and travel some. He went to Ireland, but spent much of his time stumbling around the streets of Dublin. The country was welcoming, but he could only experience so much of the singing in the pubs.

He felt alone without his friend.

So when he returned and a season passed, he went shopping for a puppy. He had saved all of Benny's toys, leashes and dog bowls. After selecting such a gentleman of a dog as Benny, James sort of saw himself as having a bit of a knack for finding a good dog. When Benny was alive, James remembered people almost seeking him out for advice on how to select a puppy. He may have not been a dog whisperer but they seemed to him to lean forward in their chairs as he explained to them convincingly the things to remain mindful of and to watch out for. He felt he had a formula. But this was not reality. Reality came when he plucked a small white puppy from the straw of a stable on a horse farm in rural Illinois on a cold March afternoon.

Toby was white like molten iron that had been poured and hardened into the mold of a dog. He was firm in his convictions and seemed impossible to change. He had been born in a manger on a horse farm in rural Illinois and until James arrived eight weeks later, had never seen direct sunlight and shared a heap of straw as bedding with eight other brothers and sisters, all with with wagging tails. He was the last of the litter to be picked.

James wasn't convinced that he was the right dog for him, but he was exhausted with his search and felt he needed to be putting himself into the service of raising a new puppy. Toby was born in a manger like Jesus but James soon began to feel that unlike Jesus, he seemed to have come from the underworld.

He was cute like all puppies, and the usual fanfare developed around the puppy presented itself when they would travel together through the streets of the town, but the innocent people who would bend down to greet him soon found that he was all claws and mouth. Then politely they would move away wishing James all the best in the raising of this dog. Of course Toby was thrilled to meet them, but he discovered that people's hands were their best tools at controlling him and he focused all his sharp teeth and mouthing on them and they would quietly withdraw. He was a true warrior who would never turn down a chance for a battle with someone's hands.

Toby was a digger. James' yard became filled with craters. His socks would appear on the lawn. Important papers were carried outside and shredded unknowingly without James' consent. His emergency brake in his truck took on a new shape and the rubber grip was textured with teeth marks. James removed all his furniture from his rooms. Closed off doors. The house became a hollow crate only the sound of the clock ticking through the halls.

But James had raised other puppies before. He knew what he was up against. He would wait out this war.

So Maybe There Is No End

So maybe there is no end to this story. Maybe stories only end when the people end and the dogs end that the people that knew those people and dogs end themselves. James was getting on in his life, age was moving him along. He had no kids and his dad was now gone, his family was scattered, and he was childless. His dogs may have or will father other puppies, who could say about that. It was starting to look as though the long line of people that had brought James to this earth was ending. He had to accept this as another reality as it had been for him to accept the death of Benny and the difference in Benny and this new dog. Some things are hard to accept and some things may never really resolve. But James was starting to see the new puppy look up at him with love in his eyes as would turn his truck around the corner of a road. It will be okay he thought, and it will be okay for him and his dog.